Of Sullied Dreams & Beaten Hearts

BY

Eidahs

Cover by

Binky Ink

Binky Ink

The literary arm of Binky Productions

www.binkyproductions.com/short stories

Table of Contents

Miles tried to control his trembling body as the shock of everything sent his mind whirling. He sat in the interrogation room, his hands clammy, unable to stare any longer at the image the detective had slapped onto the table.

It showed a bloody and gruesome depiction of Elias Stokes.

Swallowing bile, Miles turned his face away, shutting his eyes tightly. Jaw clenched, he half-whispered. 'I swear, I didn't kill him.'

'You expect me to believe that, Mister Sallow? You'll have to give me more than that.' The detective stood, pacing to and fro before him. She stopped and folded her arms, turning her head to glare down at him in contempt.

'We have empirical evidence that makes you our number one suspect.'

Miles stared up at her. He blinked. 'I honestly didn't know he was dead until you brought me in and showed me thi—' He pressed his lips together, unable to continue.

* * *

Miles awoke to loud pounding on his door.

'Miles Sallow, open up!'

'All right, all right, I'm coming, geez.' He got out of bed and took a moment to check his phone – no reply. It was time to get ready anyway for the announcement of his life.

Miles pushed his brown hair away from his forehead, taking a moment to blink any grogginess away, and his heart flipped at the thought of what today was, what today would bring.

Pulling pants on and a simple shirt for now – he'd find a dazzling outfit once he'd dealt with whoever was at the door – Miles walked over to his door, where people were still banging and shouting.

'I'm coming . . . if for no other reason than to *shut you up*!' he called out, opening the door.

Miles barely registered the police officers who stood there before he was spun around, hands pulled behind his back, and handcuffed.

'Whoa, whoa, what's going on? What the fuck *is* this?'

'Miles Sallow, you're under arrest.'

'Yeah, I gathered – the handcuffs gave it away,' he complained as they dragged him to the car. 'Can you tell me what the hell I'm being arrested for?'

'Elias Stokes.'

That was all the answer he got.

'What about Elias Stokes?' A cold sensation hit Miles's stomach. He braced his shoulder against the car, refusing to enter. 'What about him? Where is he?' Miles pushed against the shoving cops, shouting out. 'Where's Elias? What happened to Elias?!'

* * *

The drive to the station had been agony, but less than the agony Miles was in now.

The detective slapped her hands onto the table, leaning forward menacingly. 'Mister Sallow,' she scolded, 'you and Mister Stokes were rival boxers. A witness saw you leaving his apartment the night the murder took place, leaving his place a complete mess, described to be walking out with a proud smirk on your face.'

Yeah, Miles had the proudest smirk on his face then.

'We have photographic proof of you arguing with Mister Stokes several nights before the murder, and an *audio* recording a couple of days later of you *threatening* Mister Stokes. And now you sit here claiming you didn't kill him?'

* * *

Miles grinned at the interviewer in front of her loud crowd. He loved the spotlight and this crowd was rowdy – they were *swooning* for him.

'I might be the leaner boxer, but I assure you, I won't lose.'

'But you've never fought Elias Stokes before.'

Miles leaned back in the fancy chair, his grin widening, 'When has that stopped me from winning before? Sure, sure, I've lost a few matches. A champion can only rise when he has worthy opponents, am I right?'

The crowd cheered raucously.

'I'll be meeting my rival for the first time in the ring and I can assure you, he's going down!'

Miles stood, flexing his biceps for the crowd who whooped and whistled at him. Lights flashed as photographers captured the pose Miles was holding for them. He winked at one of them and blew him a kiss. Whether the men he flirted with were gay or not, they loved the attention he gave them for their articles and encouraged his flirtiness. Miles always leaned into that.

'Elias Stokes is going down!' Miles roared. 'I'm gonna *kill it* in that ring!'

* * *

The detective pushed away from the table, looking exasperated. She took the picture and shoved it in Miles's face, shouting.

'Three stab wounds to the chest, sliced throat, and a note stuffed into his mouth. If that's not personal . . . And you had every reason to want him dead.'

'I swear, I didn't kill him,' cried Miles. 'I swear it. Please, believe me. I wouldn't . . . kill . . . Elias.' His voice petered out, cracking.

'Why? Give me one good reason why you wouldn't kill your rival!'

* * *

Miles wiped the sweat off his brow, seething at his loss. 'Fuck!' he shouted. He paced to and fro in his dressing room. 'I promised the crowd I'd win this match.'

'We can work this angle with the tabloids,' said Larry. The older man stood with his arms folded, rubbing his chin thoughtfully as he leaned against the wall. 'You have a vendetta now. Revenge will be sweeter than the initial victory could have ever been.' The publicist pushed away from the wall. 'Your fans are gonna love it. It'll be bigger than when you came out as gay.'

'You think?' Miles shook his arms, 'I let my fans down.' He sighed, jumping and shaking his legs.

'You didn't let them down, Miles.' Larry looked at his watch. 'All right, I've got calls to make regarding this.' He started for the dressing room door. He looked back at Miles, pointing at him. 'We're going to spin this. It's going to be beautiful, you'll see. I'll call you tomorrow.'

Miles waved noncommittally. He shook his head, murmuring to himself. 'You think yourself such a hotshot, tough guy? I'm gonna give you a piece of my mind.'

Miles stormed out of his dressing room and right into his rival's, marching right up to him.

The tattooed boxer grinned at him. 'Come for round two?'

'Yeah, you bet.' Miles sized him up and down. 'You're going down next time.'

'You talk a big game, Miles Sallow, but we both know you couldn't put your money where your mouth was tonight.' Elias took a step forward – Miles became aware of how close and imposing his large muscles were.

'I'll have you know I *am* a big game,' Miles taunted. Elias chuckled. 'And I'll put a lot more than money in my mouth.' Miles realised what that sounded like, but he didn't care. Everyone knew he was gay anyway, so he just went with it and offered Elias a wink.

Elias inclined his head to the side, taking another step forward. 'Is that so?' He placed a finger under Miles's chin, tilting it up slightly. The touch sent a tremor down Miles's chest. 'And what do I have to do to make sure I'm the one in your mouth?'

Miles's breath hitched as Elias leaned forward. 'You're gay?' Miles looked up into his rival's eyes.

'I have to admit, before tonight, I was uncertain of what kind of boxer you'd wind up being against me.' Elias grazed his fingers along Miles's jawline. 'There is something graceful about the way you fight.' His fingers continued down Miles's bare chest. 'Maybe I can let you take the win over me in here.'

'You do realise I was set on confronting you and fighting you again?' Miles whispered.

Elias chuckled. 'I don't know why you have it in for me – how did our rivalry begin anyway? But I've always had a thing for you.'

'That's news to me,' admitted Miles, his heart racing. 'I thought you said you were going to slap me with the win so hard it was going to knock me out.'

Elias got in close to Miles's ear and whispered, his hot breath making him tingle. 'Let me rephrase: I'm going to slap you with the win,' he pressed himself against Miles, letting him feel his bulge, 'and stick it so far deep in your ass, it's going to knock you out real good with how fucking good it's going to be.'

Miles felt his legs weaken and a moan escaped his lips.

He took a beat to recompose himself. 'Who's talking a big game now?' Miles taunted, bringing his lips close to Elias's.

The other man stared at him, his eyes dark with desire. They were both still high on adrenaline, sticky with dry sweat, chests heaving, and so fucking hot for each other – Miles had never realised how sexy Elias was this up close when he wasn't fighting him in the ring.

Together, they lunged forward, a grapple to touch their faces, a hook to grab each other's asses, lips devouring and tongues thrusting into each other's mouths. Stomach flipping in so many ways, pelvis tightening, Miles and Elias wrestled for control before both succumbed to their desires.

* * *

'Answer me!' shouted the detective, bringing Miles back to the interrogation room.

The door swung open and in walked another detective, a tall tawny man with square glasses. 'Amanda, please, one question at a time.'

She sighed, looking over at her partner. 'What have you got for me?'

Instead of answering, the other detective addressed Miles, keeping his eyes on him. 'Mister Miles Sallow, I am Detective Guillermo Sanchez. You've met my fiery counterpart, Miss Amanda Cushing.'

Miles glared at them both.

Detective Sanchez pulled a chair out and sat down at the table. He flipped the photo over to its reverse side.

'You and Mister Stokes had a personal relationship, did you not?'

'The only relationship they had was one of rivalry and pure hatred.' Detective Cushing narrowed her eyes.

'That's not true!' Miles pleaded.

He clamped up his mouth as a wave of nausea hit him. Detective Sanchez gently placed another photo on the table, one of the note found in Elias's mouth. Miles couldn't bear to look at the image of the note, the words written on them were too raw for him still.

'Mister Sallow,' Sanchez began in a calm tone, 'we'd like to find the real killer, so anything you can tell us will bring us one step closer to achieving justice and releasing you. I'm going to present the evidence we found and I need your honesty. Will that work?'

Miles nodded, swallowing.

'Why are you being sympathetic towards the suspect?' demanded Cushing.

'Because our "suspect" has plausible deniability,' Sanchez replied matter-of-factly. He looked over at Miles. 'Don't you, Mister Sallow?'

Tears filled Miles's eyes. He turned around and lunged for the garbage can in the corner, vomiting into it, his entire body shaking with cold sweats.

'For Christ's sake,' complained Cushing.

Miles coughed, sobbing and retching into the garbage. Breathing heavily above it, he waited before another wave overtook him. Then he rose, wiping his mouth with his sleeve.

'If your goal was to break me, Detective Cushing, then consider yourself successful,' seethed Miles. 'But I swear on my life, I did not kill Elias Stokes.'

<u>PART 2</u>

Miles walked back to the table and sat down.

'Why should I believe you?'

Miles attempted to quell the trembling. It was Detective Sanchez who answered.

'Because Mister Sallow was in a relationship with the victim.'

'Oh, so just because he was fuck—'

'It wasn't fucking! It wasn't screwing, it wasn't sex! We were in love!' shouted Miles.

* * *

Miles lay in bed, Elias hovering above him on his side, gently stroking Miles's chest and smiling.

'We have to stop meeting like this,' chuckled Miles.

'I rather like our encounters,' protested Elias.

'I meant in secret.' Miles cupped Elias's cheek. 'I want to be able to see more of you.'

'You would?' Elias turned his face away.

'Of course I would'

'I'm not ready to come out.'

'I understand,' said Miles, interlacing his hand with Elias's. 'Imagine the tabloids, though, considering we once hated each other.'

'Did we, though?' asked Elias. 'It was all based on what the tabloids fuelled, and then we rolled with the punches.'

'I much rather roll with you,' grinned Miles.

'Miles.' Elias sobered. Miles was hit with a pang of worry. 'There's something I need to tell you.'

Miles propped himself up on his elbows. 'What is it?'

Elias passed a hand through his dark hair. He chuckled. 'Fuck, I didn't realise this would be so hard.'

Miles held his breath. 'Elias, if you want to stop seeing me, then just say so.'

'What? No, fuck no. Fuck, what am I doing?' Elias, eyes wide, took both of Miles's hands in his. 'Miles, I think I'm falling in love with you.' Miles gaped at Elias. 'No, actually, I know it. I love you.'

The surprise turned into a wide smile on Miles's face. 'I love you too.'

'You do?'

'Yeah. Fuck, I got so scared just now. Elias, I'm so fucking in love with you, I don't know what to do with myself.'

Elias's lips were back on Miles. 'Then do me. It's time for round two.'

Wrapping his arms around Elias, Miles pulled him down to him for another round of mind-blowing lovemaking.

* * *

'A crime of passion, then,' insisted Cushing. 'Let me guess, one of you wanted out? Wanted to break up?'

'No, the only disagreement we ever had was he didn't want us *to be* out.'

'Is that what you were arguing about in this photo?' inquired Detective Sanchez.

The photo showed Elias seething in Miles's face, and Miles looking aghast and dismayed – a paparazzi must've snuck in near the end of their argument to get the scoop. To an outsider, it would look like Miles would want to get back at being thrown off guard in an argument, but that wasn't it.

* * *

Miles stood with Elias in his dressing room, anticipation mounting.

'So what's this important news you wanted to tell me about so urgently?' asked Miles. He could hear the eagerness and nervousness in his voice.

'I spoke with my coach,' said Elias. 'I'm going to come out to the world. I'm going to announce that I'm gay.'

Miles beamed at Elias. 'That's fantastic. I'm so happy to hear that. How are you feeling?' Miles tucked a strand of his lover's hair behind his ear.

'I'm eager to get it done, to be honest. This has been a long time coming.'

Miles looked at him, hopeful. 'And then we don't have to hide anymore. Rivals to lovers. It'll be huge!'

'Actually,' Elias sobered, and Miles couldn't help fear Elias didn't quite feel the same way he did about this, 'I think it's best we continue to keep our relationship a secret.'

'What? Why?' demanded Miles, dropping his hands to his sides. 'Is this because of what I found? You don't want to be associated with that?'

'No, that has nothing to do with it. I just think one announcement at a time, you know?'

'You or your coach?' demanded Miles. He leaned forward. 'Why would you want to continue to hide our relationship? I don't understand. It would be a big bang.'

'I'm not like you when it comes to announcements, Miles,' insisted Elias. 'I'm more subdued.'

Elias took Miles's hands in his, rubbing his thumbs on his knuckles, but the gesture did not bring Miles any comfort.

'Then what is it? Because from where I'm standing it looks like you don't want the world to know we're seeing each other and gay together, and you're refusing to tell me why.'

'I told you.'

'That's a bullshit answer and you know it,' spat Miles. 'You love the limelight as much as I do, you revel in it in the ring. So why hide *me*? What else are you hiding?'

'Nothing, I swear.'

Miles pulled away from Elias, jerking his hands away and taking a step back. 'Oh my god, are you ashamed of me?'

'What would make you think that?!' Elias tried to extend an arm towards Miles who backed away again, pulling his hand out of reach.

'Because *I* want to shout it at the top of my lungs to the entire world that I'm in love with Elias Stokes and I want—' Miles stopped himself before he said too much. 'Do you not love me anymore?'

'What are you talking about? Of course, I still love you,' pleaded Elias. 'I'm the one who said it first, remember? I love you! What insane idea has made you think I don't?'

'Well then, there's only one other reason you would want to keep our relationship under wraps.' Miles folded his arms, his heart pounding at a thousand miles per hour, fear gripping him.

'Really? You're really going there?' Elias's face contorted. 'You think I'd cheat on you?'

'You tell me.' Miles spread out his arms in frustration. 'All this sneaking around, not wanting anyone to know about me, even when you're planning on telling the world you're gay.' Miles turned his head to the side, tears stinging his eyes.

'If you really want to think that, then I don't know what else to say?'

Miles snapped his head back at Elias. 'You're not even going to defend yourself, argue against it, prove me wrong?'

'What do you want me to say, Miles?' shouted Elias.

'That you love me!' Miles pointed at himself. 'That you'd never cheat on me!' Miles pleaded, 'That you'd do anything and everything for me. That you love me so much you . . . you want people to know so we can be together in public.'

'Well tough, Miles. We don't all think or feel the same way. It might be easy for you, but not for me.'

'Love is supposed to be easy,' Miles whimpered.

'I'm talking about being publicly gay!' shouted Elias. He huffed. 'You know what, forget it. Telling you was a mistake. I need some space.' Elias started heading out.

'Some space? From me?' Miles went after him.

'Yes!' Elias spun around to seethe in Miles's face.

Miles's vision blurred with tears. 'So now we're over?'

'Think what you wanna think, Miles, you seem to have decided everything about this anyway.'

'Elias, I'm sorry. I got overly excited, but you're right, this is your announcement, and if you want to do two separate announcements—'

'Forget it, there's nothing to announce anymore.'

'What!'

Elias turned to go. Miles reflexively grabbed his arm, pulling him back. 'Please, don't go.'

'We're done here, Miles. I can't talk to you like this.'

'Elias, please,' Miles begged, 'I love you!'

Elias paused, then jerked his hand away from Miles. Miles's breath shook at the gesture, fear making it difficult to breathe.

'Do you not love me?' Elias gave no reply. 'Elias?'

'Goodnight, Miles.' Elias left the room.

Miles let out a shaking sob, bringing his hands to his head and grabbing his hair, shielding his eyes with his elbows as fresh tears poured down his face.

Part 3

'Okay, so you had a lover's spat,' began Cushing, 'but why did you threaten the vic?'

Detective Cushing played a recording of the threat in question.

Don't you dare walk away from me.

Don't touch me.

I'm not letting you do this, I'm gonna keep coming after you. I don't care what you say or do, Elias, I won't let you walk away from this.

It sent Miles right back to that moment.

* * *

Miles marched up to Elias who was strolling beneath an overpass. It was late, it was dark, but Miles didn't care, he was going to catch him before he went home, set on trying to understand what was going on.

'Miles, what are you doing here?' Elias quavered. It was hard to see his face but the glint in his eyes tugged at Miles's heart.

'I came to find you.'

'Out here? Out in public?'

'If you can call late at night under an overpass public, then yeah, out in public.'

'Why?' demanded Elias.

'You know why!' Miles furrowed his brows in sadness as the ache in his chest squeezed harder. 'Why are you doing this, Elias? I know you love me. Why are you walking away from us like this? Do I mean nothing to you?'

Elias turned his face away. 'I've said all I had to say already.' Elias turned to go.

'Don't you dare walk away from me.' Miles grabbed Elias's arm.

Elias pulled away immediately. 'Don't touch me.'

'I'm not letting you do this, I'm gonna keep coming after you.' Miles called after him. 'I don't care what you say or do, Elias, I won't let you walk away from this.'

* * *

'What about the witness who saw you exiting your supposéd boyfriend's apartment, and why did she see everything a mess in there?' demanded Cushing.

* * *

Elias swung the door open, his face one of utter shock. 'Miles!'

Miles pushed past him, entering the apartment, scared but determined. Elias shut the door behind him. Miles turned to face him.

'I'm not giving up on us, Elias. I don't care how many times you push me away or walk away from me, I'm just not going to let you throw away what we've got without a fight.'

'And yet you let me walk away the other night.'

'Because you seemed mortified to be talking to me in public, outside in the dark where *no one* could see us. What did you want me to do? Get on my knees and beg? Because I will!' Miles took a step forward, leaning closer. Elias turned his face away. 'What is this, Elias? I thought we had something special.'

'Then why didn't you fight for me the other night?' shouted Elias, a plea behind his glaring eyes.

'I did! I respected that you didn't want me doing anything out there. What were you expecting me to do, anyway?'

Elias hesitated. 'It would have been nice to see you defy my own defiance.'

Miles scowled. 'Were you testing me?' He couldn't believe it. 'What did you expect me to do?' Elias turned away again. 'This?'

Miles grabbed Elias's wrist and pulled him back to him hard, his lips capturing the other man's. One hand cupping the back of Elias's neck, his other hand travelled down his back as he kissed him with all the longing he'd been feeling.

Elias returned the kiss fiercely before pulling away with a sob.

'Is that what you wanted me to do? Take the choice away from you . . . away from your coach, and just be with you out there to prove myself to you?'

Elias put a hand to his mouth, tears on his face. 'Miles, I just want to be out and get it over with. I don't care anymore about what looks like what. I . . . so many people have walked away from me before. I needed to know you were for real.'

'I *am* for real, Elias, and it hurts that you would test me like that. What do I need to do to prove to you how real my love is for you? What do you want me to do?'

'Sometimes I just need you to take charge!' cried Elias.

'I've been trying to respect you, that's why I haven't taken charge in this matter. Because when I did, you pushed me away.'

'I'm sorry, Miles. I'm sorry I was contradictory.'

'I love you, I'll prove it. I love you so much I don't know what to do with myself! But what about you, huh? I am so hurt right now. What are you going to do to prove your love for me? Because all I feel right now is tested and not trusted.'

Elias pushed Miles briskly to the wall, backing him up to the small mirror that loosened and fell to the floor, shattering. Hand pressed against Miles's chest, Elias's mouth devoured his lips. Miles moaned into him before Elias pulled away, his lips a hair's breadth from Miles's.

'I love you, okay!' shouted Elias. 'I, Elias Stokes, am in love with you, Miles Sallow.' He grabbed Miles by the collar, pulling and pushing, and pinned him to the table, knocking glasses down and shattering those too.

Tears poured down both their faces as they screamed at each other declarations of love and dares to prove it. They were naked and sweating before they had shouted their next declaration. Miles could feel his body tremble from sheer euphoria and adrenaline.

'You're not bending me over?' he asked.

'I want us to stare into each other's eyes as we—'

And their lips were back on each other's, moaning and declaring their love once more as their passion culminated on the table.

* * *

Miles could hardly bear it anymore. Thankfully, the door to the interrogation room opened, interrupting the detectives.

They stepped out for a few minutes, leaving Miles alone with his thoughts.

* * *

Miles lay on his stomach on top of Elias who stroked his hair gently.

'So what are you going to do regarding what you found?'

Miles sighed. 'I don't know. There are a few approaches and I know what the right thing to do is. I just want to make sure I've got everything correct before I make any moves, you know.'

'I understand.'

'This could ruin my career, but I don't care. I'm going to do the right thing.'

'And I'm going to support you through it.' Elias smiled, more sheepishly than anything else. 'Well, talk about layoffs, I fired my coach.'

Miles's brows shot up. 'You did?'

'Yeah.' Elias chuckled. 'He was the one who kept pushing me to delay any announcements, who wanted my relationship with you kept secret. I took everything he said at face value – his reasons made sense at the time — but when I started changing my mind and questioning what *I* really wanted, he started getting nasty with me.'

Elias shook his head. Miles cupped his face.

'I confronted him earlier. Turns out he was worried about *his* public image . . . being associated . . . with . . .' Elias pressed his lips together – Miles could guess what this was about. ' "People like us." '

Miles hissed. 'What a fucking bigot.'

'I know. I told him the fuck off, and fired his ass.' Elias met Miles's gaze.

'What are you going to do now without him?'

Elias shrugged. 'I don't need him, Miles. As long as I have you, that's all I'll ever need.'

He wrapped his arms around Miles, pressing a gentle kiss to his lips. Miles breathed in elatedly, intoxicated by the scent of his lover's musky sweat. He wrapped his arms around him too, relaxing in Elias's arms.

* * *

The detectives returned. They walked back to the table, silent, and sat down across Miles.

'Our comrades have searched your place. They found this.' Detective Sanchez placed the small ring box on the table.

Miles pressed his lips together, trembling as more tears threatened to spill.

'I bought that after we reconciled,' he managed.

* * *

Weeping quietly, the two boxers held each other on the couch, having moved away from the table – their bodies were sticky with sweat, but the heat radiating from Elias comforted Miles.

'I'm sorry,' whispered Elias.

Miles stroked his hair. 'So am I.' He let out a small laugh. 'What are we like? You drive me insane?'

'And you don't?'

'Elias, I love you so much I don't know what to do with myself. I don't want a future without you. I want to spend the rest of my life with you!' Miles stopped, realising what he'd said.

Elias shifted, gazing deep into Miles's eyes so intensely it nearly made him orgasm. 'What did you just say?' he asked softly.

Miles dove right in – either he'd drown or Elias would pull him up and say yes.

'Elias, I don't want a future without you, I want to marry you. If that's the proof you need, I'll get on my knees and propose.'

Miles slid off Elias and onto the floor, onto his knees, taking Elias's hands in his. The tight ache in his heart eased mildly as he gazed into his lover's eyes with renewed hope.

'I'll get you the biggest fucking ring, the *best* fucking diamond ring I can find. I'll fly helicopter banners for you. Elias, I want to spend the rest of my life with you. And all I need from you, is a yes, and it's all yours. *I'm* already all yours.'

'Yes. Yes so many fucking times, yes. Yes, Miles. Fuck yes, I want to marry you!'

Miles could not hold back his happy tears. He let out a tearful laugh of joy.

'Fuck, Elias!' He rose and pressed his lips to his lover's. 'I'm going to fucking marry you.'

'You're gonna get me a ring then, yes? You're gonna get it tomorrow?'

'I promise it'll be worth the wait. I love you.' Miles beamed at Elias, whose smile made his heart burst with love.

'I love you too. I'm sorry I got so hot-headed.'

'I'm sorry I jumped to conclusions,' said Miles, giving him a wan smile.

'Well, I wasn't helping, to be fair, I just . . .' Elias held Miles's face in his hands. 'I love you so much it scares me sometimes, but I want the world to know about us. I do want to announce we're together.'

Miles's heart somersaulted with happiness.

'So let's make it special,' Elias went on. 'Let's announce our engagement together. And yeah, let's make it the biggest announcement in the world.'

Elias mimicked calling out to his fans in his stoic voice. 'Hey Stokesers, guess what? I'm gay and I'm getting married to Miles Sallow, my rival in the ring and partner in bed. He is the man I love, I am *in love* with him, and I don't want to hide it anymore.'

Miles laughed as Elias continued in a more exaggerated tone, louder this time.

'I'm gay and in love with Miles Sallow and we're gonna keep competing against each other because it's our biggest fucking turn-on!'

Miles aligned himself better, kissing Elias as they both chuckled. Miles felt again more of that wonderful sensation in his stomach and pelvis.

'*You're* my fucking turn-on,' he whispered huskily.

They made love again before Miles finally left to buy his *fiancé* his ring. He tucked it in a safe place at his apartment, looking forward to giving it to Elias in the morning. Miles would have preferred to spend the night with him, but since the press would be arriving early in the morning, he'd let Elias introduce their announcement before the charity event.

Miles would prepare the best fucking proposal. Elias had promised the best fucking announcement. Their fans were going to go wild with this announcement and they both loved that.

'But I love you more than any thrill in the world,' they had both declared.

<u>PART 4</u>

Sanchez placed the receipt on the table. 'This places you at the store at the time of the murder.'

Miles waited for relief to wash over him but instead, his heart only dropped further.

'Well, it seems you have an alibi, Mister Sallow,' Cushing conceded.

'You're free to go,' said Sanchez.

'Free to go?' Miles felt the anger rise within him. 'Go where? Back to my apartment? Alone?' Now he shouted, pointing outside. 'When the man I love lies dead and the killer is out there?'

The two detectives looked at each other.

Miles lowered his voice. 'You might as well just keep me here because now all I want to do is top myself.'

'Mister Sallow, making suicidal threats in front of police detectives—'

'What my partner means to say,' interrupted Sanchez, 'is we're very sorry for your loss.'

'Bullshit!' Miles stood abruptly. 'You're not sorry at all. You're disappointed that you haven't got the killer when you were so convinced it was me.' Miles shook his head. 'You know what? Screw it. Screw *this*. Screw both of you!'

'Mister Sallow,' said Sanchez as Miles began towards the door. Miles stopped. 'Is there anyone you know who might have wanted Elias Stokes dead?'

Miles thought about it but his mind came up blank. 'No.' He bowed his head. 'Can I leave now?'

* * *

'Elias Stokes versus Miles Sallow!' the announcer boomed. 'Both certainly have scores to settle with each other. And after an exciting first round, which one of them will come out on top?'

Miles and Elias grappled each other, butting foreheads and pushing against the other. The crowd roared and cheered, camera flashes went off.

'You can't do that,' Miles complained in a whisper. 'I just want your lips right now.' Elias only grinned in reply.

'These rivals are in a lover's lock,' the announcer continued. 'Will they ever kiss and make up, or will their rivalry bring one of them down?'

Miles pushed away, bringing his gloved hands up and going for an uppercut. Elias blocked, feigned, and went to punch low. Miles foresaw but had not foreseen the second feint within the first feint, and he fell onto his back.

'Looks like Elias is dominating the famed Miles.'

Elias bent down, grinning cheekily. Miles grabbed his head within his thighs, locking him in place.

'Fuck,' breathed Elias. 'I am so fucking turned on right now.'

'This isn't wrestling, gentlemen. Will Miles be given a penalty?'

Miles opened up his legs, kicking Elias back as the other boxer stood, before rising to his feet himself. Elias bounced off the edge of the ring, still grinning. Miles's eyes darted to his bulge, seeing just how much his lover was turned on right now.

Thinking Elias was shaking himself to refocus, Miles let his guard down – on purpose – turning his back to him. Elias was pressing against him and whispering harshly in his ear within seconds.

'We need to end this now. I want you too fucking badly.'

Miles chuckled, turning around, as Elias backed away. Miles winked at him and blew him a kiss before passing a hand over his bare and sweaty chest.

The crowd went crazy, as did the announcer. Their flirt dance in the ring was the best foreplay Miles had ever known. Elias jabbed the air and thrust a gloved fist in a side uppercut motion, glaring at Miles seductively.

I'm going to fist you, is what it meant. *I'm going to take you from behind.*

Miles bucked his hips in response.

'They're doing their ritual of threats,' the announcer roared in glee and amusement. 'Someone is about to get it, and about to get it hard.'

Back in his dressing room, Miles wiped sweat from his face with a wet towel. Elias barged in, slamming the door behind him.

'Fuck, babe, you had me seeping in the ring.' His large tattooed arms reached for Miles, pulling him in fast for a hungry kiss. Miles felt like his legs would give out beneath him – he always did.

'You were taunting me, baby, I had to even the playing field.' Miles felt his and his lover's readiness for their ritualistic romp in the dressing room as they continued to devour each other's mouths.

Elias pulled away from the kiss to go and lock the door. When he walked back, he wrapped his arms around Miles from behind, pressing his entire body to his.

'These mirrors turn me so the fuck on, Miles. I want to see you from every angle.'

'Take me, baby. Oh, fuck, Elias, do good on that promise you made in the ring.'

They were naked within a minute, and Elias and Miles had their arms wrapped around each other again, lips locked and wrestling for control of the other's tongue.

Miles jumped up onto the counter and wrapped his legs around Elias.

'Lock your thighs around my head again and I will do what I wanted to out there.' Elias's voice was so husky, that Miles slid down further as he sat there, melting for Elias.

'And then I'll do good on that promise and take you from behind.'

Chuckling, the two boxers made love – another round of passionate and mind-blowing sex in the dressing room after a match. Whether it was against each other or another, they always found each other in their dressing rooms for a few rounds of their own. They were always so hot and so ready for each other. And then they would continue at either of their apartments when they could.

* * *

Miles swung the door open and paused right before exiting the interrogation room. He spoke low, 'Can I see him?'

Miles followed Sanchez to the morgue, feeling numb the whole time. He needed to see Elias, he needed confirmation that this was real, that it wasn't just some bad dream. Or more, perhaps, he was hoping it *was* a bad dream, just a huge mistake, and Elias was alive after all. But even as he thought it, the feeling of sinking ever deeper into an ocean of sorrow told him how real this all was.

Miles was trembling from head to toe when the mortician removed the sheet covering Elias. Miles braced himself as he looked upon his lover's tranquil face, the gash on his neck cleaned, and Miles felt the blood drain from his face.

He put a hand to his mouth, sobbing uncontrollably – he felt as though his heart was being ripped apart at the sight of Elias's dead body.

He quavered, his voice increasing in intensity, his body folding in on itself as the shock overtook him anew, 'Oh god, oh god, Elias, oh god, baby, oh god!'

Weakness overwhelmed Miles – his legs gave way and he fell. Sanchez caught him before he could hit the ground.

Miles screamed for Elias, his hysteria tearful, his body limp in the officer's grip, and unable to control the flow of his sorrow. A desperate wail escaped him, and the ache in his heart killed him inside.

* * *

Miles stared at the chef's knife in his hand. It wasn't exactly shaped like the one used to kill Elias, based on the photo of the stab wounds, but he supposed it would do. He'd sharpened it, tested it on the tip of his finger. It felt heavy, and the blade cold.

He was so angry, so hurt, so confused. All he wanted was to see Elias again, and there was only one way that could happen. He wanted to die the way Elias had.

Steeling himself, he brought the knife up.

His hand trembled so much he couldn't hold the knife to his throat, so he tried aligning it with his heart. He wondered how hard of a push he'd have to give before his body instinctively stopped him from sheer pain or reflex.

A thud pulled him out of his musings. He refocused but heard the thud again, and then . . . footsteps.

Wielding the knife he'd intended to use on himself, Miles spun around to face the midnight intruder. A masked figure all in black, someone who wielded a knife that matched the stab wounds on Elias's body.

Miles shouted in alarm, taking a step back and lifting his own knife. His attacker thrust forward and Miles sidestepped. He kneed his attacker in the stomach and followed through with an uppercut. He jabbed the knife but the intruder stabbed down and Miles reflexively moved his hand away.

His opponent grabbed Miles's wrist, pushing him back, and jerked his arm up, hitting it hard against the wall. Miles dropped his knife. One hand still free, Miles punched his attacker in the stomach and off him before the assailant's knife could come at his throat.

Fighting for his life, adrenaline coursing through his body, Miles realised he wanted to live, despite feeling a part of him had died with Elias that morning. He wanted to be alive right now at least, so he could kill the man who'd killed his lover.

Miles punched his attacker in the face and kicked him in the balls so hard, the intruder fell onto his back. Miles got on top of him, pinning him to the ground, and pulled the masked hood off his assailant.

The face he looked down at sent a shockwave of fear through his body.

'You!' he gasped. 'You weren't after Elias, were you? You were after me!'

'He was collateral. Sorry.'

Miles seethed. 'You're not sorry.'

Miles walked out of the studio, overhearing the whispers from those who had done his makeup. It unnerved him. Why would they think he was sketchy as fuck?

Some of the things they said didn't make sense. So Miles decided to look into the books, something just didn't add up.

He looked over the accounts. Money sent to one magazine, money to another, money to news outlets – all places he had done interviews for.

He tallied the totals. He checked the charities and bank receipts, calling banks and poring over the numbers for hours, trying to piece it together. That's where he found it.

The charity report said one million to one charity and the collected money said one million – the charity had indeed received one million – but then there were two transactions to two different bank accounts of one additional million each. Three million. When Miles looked over at the extra totals from earlier? Two million. And they were all signed in the same name.

'Larry, you fucking—' he muttered to himself.

Miles met with his publicist the next day, acting casual so as to not raise suspicion.

'What's up, Miles? What do you want my magic to do for you today?'

'Actually, I've decided to go indie,' said Miles.

'Indie?' Larry creased his brows, puzzled.

'Yeah, it's the big trend these days and fans are all over it, they want indie artists and celebs. So, like . . . I no longer need your services.'

'Come on, Miles, you need me.'

'Well, I want to try this for a bit, you know. Get on the Internet social media trends, do interviews with more down-to-earth folks. People are gonna love it. It's what I want to give them too.'

'Are you sure?'

'Yeah.'

'So you're basically firing me, that it?' asked Larry, matter-of-factly.

'Yeah, kind of.' Miles hesitated, biting his lip, trying to figure out how to play this one out.

'All right, but when you change your mind or you realise that indie stuff isn't cutting it anymore,' Larry pointed at Miles, 'you call me.'

'You bet, Larry. Thanks for understanding, and for all you've done.'

Larry snapped a finger and pointed it again at Miles as he backed away. Miles sighed internally. He needed to gather the necessary information before figuring out what to do next. But first, he had a heart to win back.

* * *

'Why, Larry? Why did you try to kill me?'

'Oh, for crying out loud, Miles, you know why! I knew the moment you fired my ass that you knew.'

Miles was trembling, he could barely hold Larry down. Despite this, Miles had the advantage – Larry was a big man, but he was no boxer.

'Did you know about me and Elias?'

'I didn't even know it *was* Elias when I did it.'

Tears stung Miles's eyes. He pressed down harder on Larry's throat, squeezing in rage. Larry croaked beneath him. Miles's life had been on the line and he just wanted to end the one who'd killed the man he loved.

Voice hoarse and wet with sorrow, Miles screamed in rage. 'Explain to me how you fucking killed my fiancé by accident!'

'Fiancé?' Larry's eyes widened, his voice filled with the sarcasm that told Miles he had known. 'Wow, congratulations.'

'FUCK YOU!'

Miles reached for his knife, wanting to make Larry pay in the most gruesome way possible, but moving was a mistake. Larry rolled over onto his stomach away from Miles and grabbed *his* knife. He rolled back and kicked Miles's hand. Miles cried out, plunging the knife down hard. He hit the floor with it and Larry moved to get on top of him, pinning him onto his stomach.

Miles punched backwards to no avail. Larry grabbed Miles's arms in a more expert manoeuvre than a mere publicist should know, and pressed down on Miles, sliding his knife beneath his throat.

Miles stopped all movement, calculating that if he tried anything, he was dead and Larry would get away. He had to kill Larry if it was the last thing he did.

'You want to know what happened, right?' Larry seethed into Miles's ear. 'I'll give you that. I knew I had to get rid of you, so I planned it out, how to bypass security, everything, except you weren't home the night I wanted to kill you. I followed you and saw you enter someone's place.'

Larry pressed the knife just a tad harder. Miles was *this* tempted to push down to finish the job, if not for wanting to hear Larry's explanation.

'I trusted you, Larry.'

'Until you didn't anymore. You were going to land me in jail, it was just a matter of time – days if I was lucky, hours if I wasn't.' Larry seethed. 'Years of hard work and deals.'

'Years of fraud and embez— Argh!'

Larry repositioned himself – the strain on Miles's pulled-back arms sent jolts of pain to his shoulders, and Miles cried out.

'You had to be fucking good to find it all and I could read it on your face that you did. I wasn't going to let you thwart me. After my first failed attempt, I saw you were biding your time. I knew I could plan this out better.'

'Then I should have reported you immediately!' countered Miles.

'Except you know as well as I do from everything I've taught you that you would have been a suspect, questioned, your reputation on the line, and anyone associated with you possibly ruined just as much as you. I saw you were calculating your next move. So I calculated mine. Thanks by the way, for giving me a few extra days to end you.'

'You're. Fucking. Welcome.'

Larry chuckled in a way that made Miles gag.

'So back to last night,' continued Larry, 'I found a way to enter the apartment and hid until the lights were out.'

'Yeah, except I was already gone by that time.'

'You must've left when my eyes weren't on the front anymore. I snuck to the bed in the dark and went for the throat first. Then I realised it wasn't you. I stabbed a few times to make it look like someone was angry at the tattooed and naked man in that bed. I saw the note you wrote and shoved it in his mouth. At least you'd get sent down and no one would believe you after this if I didn't get my hands on you first.'

'Why didn't you come finish the job last night, at my place?' demanded Miles.

'Oh, but I did, except your neighbours were having a party that lasted all night and people were in and out smoking and drinking by the doorway. There was no way no one would miss me.'

'And then I got arrested and you thought I'd get sent down for *your* crime!'

'Simple as that.'

'Do it, then. Finish me, Larry. Make it as clean as you did with Elias. I can't wait to spend the rest of my afterlife with him.'

'As you wish, Miles. It's been a fun ride, thank you. I'll disappear and—'

The door to Miles's place burst open and a gunshot rang through the air. The knife beneath Miles's throat dropped and Larry fell to the side with a thud. When Miles looked back, there was a hole in the publicist's chest and he was bleeding out, eyes glazed over. He was dead.

Miles looked up at the two detectives who stood with guns raised at the door.

Miles shoved Larry off him and rose, staggering to where his knife still lay on the floor. Tears pouring down his face, Miles fell to his knees, and reached for his knife. It was over.

'Drop the knife, Miles.'

'Why? It's over. Whether me or you, I'm dead – I died with Elias.'

* * *

Lights flashed and cameras clicked. Miles couldn't hold their gazes, couldn't face them, he could only bow his head as his vision blurred with tears.

'I loved him so much, and we were going to get married. We were going to come out about it, he was going to announce it publicly, and we were going to announce our engagement.'

Miles shut his eyes.

A hand reached for his knee. 'I am so sorry, Miles. If there is anything we can do, anything at all, anything you need.'

'There's nothing you can do. I need *him*, I need Elias.'

And he would have liked to add, *I need to join him.*

Miles brought a hand to his eyes, sobbing uncontrollably. 'It's my fault he's dead. The killer wanted to get *me*! If I had been there, he'd still be alive.'

'But then *you'd* be dead.'

I already am.

* * *

Miles stood in his dressing room, stripped naked and staring at himself in the mirror. He took the ring he'd bought for Elias and slipped it on his finger. Then he took hold of the scrunched paper that had been stuffed in his lover's mouth and uncreased it, looking down at it as fresh tears wet it.

'That's one hell of a beautiful ring.'

Miles looked up to see Elias in the reflection, his tattooed arms reaching around him. Elias gently kissed Miles on the neck.

'I told you I'd get you the best fucking ring,' said Miles.

Elias reached down to Miles's pelvis and began to stroke. 'One last romp in the dressing room?'

'Before the curtain call.'

Elias kissed him again. The pang of arousal was at once invigorating as it was heart-wrenching. Elias was the most gorgeous man Miles had ever set his eyes on. His love was the only one Miles would ever let consume him.

Miles watched Elias in the mirror as his lover pleasured him, feeling him completely. The way his arms flexed, the smell of his breath, the sensation of his lips on his skin. Heat rose to Miles's face as he felt Elias fill him.

As ecstasy overtook him, Miles joined his lover.

* * *

Miles tucked his shirt into his pants and then grabbed the first paper he could find and started writing on it.

'What are you doing now?' Elias chuckled.

'I'm writing you a contract.' replied Miles as he wrote.

'On a piece of scrap paper with a faulty pen?'

Miles knelt before his still-naked lover. 'In anticipation for tomorrow. You're gonna get it tomorrow, I promise. As soon as your charity event is done with, I mean, we don't want to cause a scandal, but we'll do it how you want it. And this is my promise to you of how serious I am to marry you. I'm going to get you that ring tonight, and tomorrow, the whole fucking world will know how I'm the luckiest man in the entire world.'

He ripped the paper to make it smaller and placed it on Elias's chest. Bending, Miles kissed him tenderly, lingering a while before reluctantly pulling away, lest they make love all over again – round three.

'Let's do it first thing, then,' said Elias. 'Come by tomorrow morning, we'll start the event with our announcement.'

Miles's heart soared. 'You mean it?'

'My promise to you of how much I am saying yes, Miles. Wear your best outfit.'

'I will.'

'And then it won't matter who sees what when, we'll have told them before they can say peep about it. Then they can see us waking up together every day as far as I care.'

'I'll be here first thing. For the re-proposal.'

Elias laughed as did Miles. Miles kissed Elias again before backing away, torn between defying him now and wanting to get the ring and plan the best public proposal his lover deserved.

He left the apartment with a proud smirk on his face, feeling like he could fly.

* * *

They found Miles Sallow's body in his dressing room, wearing the ring, his fingers clutching the note he'd written.

I love you so much I don't know what to do with myself.

I don't want a future without you.

I want to spend the rest of my life with you.

<u>THANK YOU SO MUCH FOR READING</u>

If you enjoyed this story,
please consider taking a few moments
to write a review on Amazon or Goodreads.
It would mean so much.

Thank you.

Please enjoy this passage from

Sanguine Sincerity

The first book in an ongoing series of
Supernatural LGBTQ Erotic Romance Thriller
books.

THE EXCERPT IS CLEAN.

Warnings:
Strong language, violence and blood.

<u>Chapter One</u>

Present Day.

The silence was both terrifying and soothing at the same time. Liam closed his eyes and leaned against the brick wall as he stood outside the club. It had been busy, with people dancing, shouting, laughing, all drunkenly. Now, the stillness of the winter night dampened whatever sounds came from the boulevard a few streets down.

This was where he had often stood with Julian after their work shifts, talking, laughing, kissing, and making plans for their future together. But Julian was gone, left before dawn a few nights after they had declared their love for each other, left without a word or explanation. Only a scribble on a sticky note saying, *'I have to leave. I'm sorry.'*

It hurt, it still did, even after all these weeks. Julian had never called or answered Liam's calls or texts after that night; Julian had simply disappeared from Liam's life. Liam didn't understand why – he thought they'd been happy.

He had once relished in the quiet after the bustle of work, now he missed hearing Julian's voice or seeing his smile. His heart broke every day again and again. Yet he continued to stand here in the spot they had made theirs.

Liam couldn't help but wonder if things had moved too fast between them – no, he had declared his love six full months after they'd met and started dating. He was just so confused about it all.

Taking a deep breath, he ensured the club was well locked and began down the dark alley. He didn't want to linger too long. There had been murders in the neighbourhood in recent weeks, all gunshot wounds. The rival gangs were at it again. It hadn't stopped the clubgoers, though. Liam figured it was only a matter of time before both mobs decided they wanted to own the club and took their fight to the neighbouring streets.

Liam heard the screech of tires and shouting not too far. He paused, waiting to make sure it was just some drunk folks, but he tensed when he heard a gunshot pierce the stillness.

Looks like the gang fight's here now, he thought to himself.

He quickened his pace and veered the corner into the next alley and came face to face with the man who had left him.

'Julian!' Liam breathed. He swallowed hard, his heart suddenly drumming in his chest.

'Liam.' Julian hesitated. His blue eyes seemed brighter in the darkness of the night and the light in the alley gave his already pale complexion a blue hue, making his handsome features that much more intense, increasing the yearning and anguish in Liam's heart.

Liam was flooded by a wave of emotions. 'What the hell, Julian?' he shouted, tears stinging his eyes.

Julian winced, chagrined, and Liam saw his eyes sparkle with tears.

'Look,' began Julian, taking a step towards Liam, 'I know I owe you an explanation, I just . . . You need to get out of here. I came to get you to safety.'

Liam took a step back, putting two and two together. 'I know what this is,' he seethed. 'You're with the mafias, aren't you?'

'No, I swear, Liam! I'm not with them,' protested Julian. 'I heard about the Cromwells and Sharpes taking their fight here and I came to warn you. Liam, please.' Julian reached for Liam's hand.

Liam pulled away out of reach. 'A little convenient, isn't it?'

Julian grimaced. 'Liam, I promise you—'

'Promise me? I told you I loved you and then you ran!' shouted Liam, his voice hoarse with heartache. His heart felt tight, and it hurt all over again.

Julian merely gaped at him.

'I thought you loved me too,' Liam wept.

'I do. I do *still* love you,' insisted Julian.

'Then why did you leave?' demanded Liam.

'I had . . . priorities.' He caught himself. 'Sorry, that sounds . . . I had . . . a mission.'

'A mission?' Liam repeated, incredulous. 'Crime mission? Or are you with the cops?'

'None of those,' admitted Julian. 'Look, I promise I'll explain everything. Let's just get out of here, go somewhere safe, and I'll explain everything.' He paused and a tear trickled down his cheek – he wiped it away with the back of his thumb. 'I just ask that you trust me.'

'You left, Julian.' The tightness in Liam's chest squeezed harder. 'You claim you love me but you left – why come back now?'

Julian stared at Liam, eyes pleading. 'I had no choice, something . . . took me away for a while, and I realise I should have told you then what it was and why that was, because—'

Gunshot thundering too close for comfort interrupted their tearful exchange.

Julian grabbed Liam's hand and began to run, pulling Liam along with him. 'We have to get out of here. I'm not going to let any harm come to you.'

'Oh, how noble!' spat Liam.

Julian spun on Liam, glaring at him. 'I came back as soon as my mission was complete. I always intended to. I just couldn't tell you then and it's . . . difficult to explain, it would be difficult for you to belie—'

With surprising speed, Julian placed his hand in front of Liam and pushed him against the wall, backing up as a bullet whizzed past them.

Liam stared at Julian, mouth agape. 'Thanks.'

Julian took a beat, looking alarmed, before grabbing hold of Liam's hand again and guiding him out of the alley and bolting onto the street. Shouts coming from nearby told them which way *not* to run as they turned onto the next street over, darting as fast as they could.

Some of the mobsters ran onto the street where they were. Julian skidded to a stop, his eyes darting this way and that, looking hypervigilant. He grabbed Liam's arm and pulled him close, turning around as one of the gang members took aim at them. They ducked behind a parked car.

'We're not with the Sharpes!' Julian shouted. Liam noted how Julian had easily recognised that the ones shooting at them were the Cromwells.

In response, the shooter reloaded his gun.

'Shit!' Julian cursed. He looked towards another parked car. 'If we can get ourselves out of this area,' he told Liam, 'then we—'

The window of the car behind which they hid shattered as another shot resounded behind them.

They ran towards the next car, and then towards another building. Another thunderous roar broke the air as more gang members began shooting at each other. Liam and Julian's assailant continued after them and just as they came up to hide in an alcove, a bullet hit Julian with a thud.

He cried out in pain, bringing his hand to his arm.

'Julian!' Liam cried.

Julian closed his eyes, wincing. 'I'll be fine,' he gritted. He looked over at Liam as they leaned against the wall. 'I'm sorry I never told you the truth. I'm sorry

I left – I'm sorry I hurt you. But I swear I love you and I will tell you *everything*. We just need to get to safety.'

Liam nodded. 'You knew they were coming here. I just can't wrap my head around—'

'I found out just hours ago.' Julian looked at his wound, breathing deeply but looking like the pain wasn't as intense now as it was before. 'I got myself here as quickly as I could.'

'You came to . . . warn me . . .' Liam was just so confused. 'Please, tell me if you're part of a gang of some sort.'

'Of some sort,' Julian repeated pensively. 'Not a mafia, no. Not a . . . It's complicated.' Julian pinched his fingers and reached into his wound and pulled out the bullet with nothing more than a small groan. 'I'm good.'

Suddenly, the barrel of a handgun emerged from the corner – the shooter was pointing it straight at Julian's head, his grip on the handgun firm and steady.

Liam froze.

Julian stared the other man in the eyes. 'Big mistake,' he sneered.

With exceptional speed, he grabbed the assailant's arm, pulling and twisting. The Cromwell crony cried out, dropping the gun, and Julian grabbed his neck and twisted hard. The man fell dead on the ground before him.

Liam stared at Julian. 'And you say you're not a cop or with a mob,' he said, unconvinced. He pointed at the dead shooter, his eyes never leaving Julian's. 'Explain that!'

'Not here.'

Julian picked up the dead man's gun and began to run; Liam followed close behind. A car turned onto the street and mobsters began to shoot at anyone who was nearby.

'Fuck!' Julian shouted. Shielding Liam as they continued to run, Julian took aim and began shooting at the mobsters within the vehicle, hitting his mark every time.

'Now I know there's definitely something you're not telling me,' Liam muttered as they ran.

'There is, and I promise I'll tell you,' replied Julian. He secured the clip and aimed afresh, again not missing his target.

Liam's throat and lungs were burning but he pushed forward. They turned another corner as the car behind them crashed into a fence.

Liam stopped before Julian, facing him. 'The truth now, Julian!'

Panting, Julian stared at Liam. 'We need to get away from here,' he insisted.

'I'm not moving until you tell me what's going on.'

Fear flashed in Julian's eyes. 'You're not going to believe me without the full explanation.'

'Then quit stalling and explain already!' demanded Liam.

Julian worked his jaw. 'I'm—'

A deafening gunshot exploded – Liam felt a sharp, burning sensation in his gut, and his knees buckled beneath him as he struggled to stay upright.

'No!' screamed Julian.

He caught Liam before he could hit the ground, gently setting him down. Liam's breath came out syncopated as he realised what had just happened. He screamed in pain – a loud guttural scream – then winced, clenching his jaw.

'No, no, this is what I was trying to prevent,' Julian quavered, opening up Liam's jacket and staring at the wound. 'I can't lose you.'

'Lose me? You left me.'

Julian let out a tearful breath. 'I left on a mission I couldn't tell you about. I'm so sorry, Liam.'

Liam glanced down at his stomach as his blood rapidly drenched his clothes. Seeing it only made his heart pump harder and the blood gush faster, and Liam's breath came out shakily.

Julian pulled Liam close to his chest, picking him up off the ground, and began to run. Liam didn't know if it was the dizziness of blood loss that altered his perceptions but he felt like they were moving a lot faster than was normal. He saw houses whizz by his vision and then trees as they entered the forest. The sounds of guns and shouting mobsters grew distant until, finally, the quiet of the night was all that remained.

Julian placed Liam down on the snow, which quickly turned red from his blood. Julian's jaw was clenched.

The pain Liam felt was immeasurable, yet somehow he couldn't bring himself to scream again, and he was so sweat-soaked from fear, he barely noticed the cold.

'I should never have waited this long to tell you the truth, Liam.' Julian looked down at Liam's wound, his tears dripping onto it.

Liam tried to speak but a mere whimper escaped him as tears stung his eyes.

Julian's voice came out determined yet half-whispered. 'I'm not going to let you die.'

'I think,' Liam winced, his voice laboured, 'it's too late for that.'

'No!' Something flashed in Julian's eyes. Liam lifted a bloodied hand to Julian's face; Julian placed his hand on his. 'I came back because I love you . . . because I owe you the truth. So here is the truth.'

His eyes flashed again and paled, brightening, his pupils becoming as blue as his irises and nearly as pale. He let his mouth hang open, and smoothly his top canines extended. Liam's eyes widened and he gaped at Julian.

'You're a—' he gasped.

'Yes. I can save your life, but tell me no and I won't, as much as that grieves me. I won't force this life on you.'

Liam gritted his teeth as a wave of pain threatened to pull him into unconsciousness. 'Do it!'

Julian leaned down towards him and gently placed his teeth on his skin. He paused. Liam felt Julian's breath on his neck before an intense sting.

He winced, grabbing Julian's arm tightly. He felt Julian's lips wrap around the punctures and the pain eased. As Julian sucked his blood, Liam relaxed in his caress.

Julian kissed Liam's neck tenderly before pulling away. 'It's done,' he said softly.

Liam waited, his body trembling lightly. Then he began to shake, but not from pain, from some sort of power that coursed through his veins. It was a vibration that came from inside of him that he felt gushing through all his veins. In his mouth, Liam felt his eyeteeth extend, and there was a mild prickle in his eyes that he just knew was the same kind of flare he'd seen in Julian's eyes.

Liam looked down at his wound, feeling an uncomfortable sensation. The bullet appeared at the opening of the hole in his stomach and fell out. Then the wound closed and Liam felt himself heal inside his body. It wasn't pleasant but the discomfort quickly passed.

Liam swallowed hard, breathing in deeply. He stared at Julian.

He wasn't sure which of them sprung towards the other first but their lips met and their mouths opened to let the other in, and they kissed fervently. The familiar tingling in Liam's stomach told him how much he loved and wanted Julian.

He pulled away. Julian leaned his forehead on his.

'I am so sorry, Liam, that I never told you the truth.'

'You should have trusted that I'd believe you,' Liam placed his hand on Julian's face, 'that I'd still love you despite who or what you are.' Liam grimaced at the blood he'd smeared on Julian who didn't seem to mind.

Julian kissed Liam again. 'I love you, Liam. I promise I'll never leave your side again.'

Liam let that sink in, realising the implications of this new situation. 'I guess that means we're geared to spend eternity together.'

Julian's lips quirked into a side grin. 'Is that a proposal?'

Liam chuckled, feeling flutters all over his body. 'It is if you want it to be.'

Julian beamed at him, and with his heightened senses Liam could feel the truth and their love reverberate and pulse between them.

Liam pressed a long and ardent kiss to Julian's lips, wrapping his arms around him, deepening the kiss with each passing moment, and his tongue traced his lover's vampiric canines as they hungrily devoured each other's mouths.

Liam drew back and met Julian's gaze. 'You owe me one hell of an explanation.'

Julian let out a small laugh. 'That, I do.'

Julian helped Liam to his feet and he beckoned him to follow. He held out his hand and Liam took it, interlacing their fingers. They walked through the snow in the forest, the silence of the night no longer terrifying Liam, and Julian's voice soothingly cut through the stillness as he began his story.

Also By

Also Written by Eidahs

Sanguine Sincerity
(https://binkyproductions.com/supernaturalromance)

Like Father, Not Like Sons
Legacy Takedown
(www.binkyproductions.com/shortstories)

Also Published by Binky Ink

Stardust Destinies I: Variate Facing
Stardust Destinies II: The Drought
(https://binkyproductions.com/stardustdestinies)

Multiple Short Stories on Medium
Soon To Be Published in Book Format
(https://medium.com/@BinkyInkWriting)

Eidahs is a pseudonym for all mature written works, from thrillers to erotic romance. Eidahs in pronunciation sounds elven in nature, which is why she chose it, to tap into her love of fantasy, a genre that couples well with supernatural and preternatural, dark fantasy, and romance.

Eidahs is also the nickname 'Shadie' backwards, representing the shadow self, innermost desires, and a spectrum of emotions, most notably, passion, sorrow, rage, and delight, which Eidahs loves to incorporate in her writing. Enticing readers and evoking the characters' emotions when she writes has guided her inspiration to spell many short stories on Medium and a series of books under this pen name.

Connect with Binky Ink:

WordPress Website & Blog
    https://binkyproductions.com/binkyinkwriting
Medium – Main Profile
    https://medium.com/@BinkyInkWriting
X (Twitter) https://twitter.com/binkyinkwriting

www.ingramcontent.com/pod-product-compliance
Lightning Source LLC
Chambersburg PA
CBHW071357200726
48294CB00004B/1200